OLIVER JEFFERS

ONCE UPON AN
ALPHABET

A B C D E F
G H I J K L
M N O P Q R
S T U V W
X Y Z

HarperCollins *Children's Books*

To Dad

Thanks for never making
us get a real job.

Love Oliver and Rory

First published in hardback in Great Britain
by HarperCollins Children's Books in 2014

10 9 8 7 6 5 4 3 2 1

ISBN: 978-0-00-751427-4

Design by Rory Jeffers

HarperCollins Children's Books is a division
of HarperCollins Publishers Ltd.

Text and illustrations copyright © Oliver Jeffers 2014

Visit our website at www.harpercollins.co.uk

Printed in China

IF WORDS MAKE up STORIES, and LETTERS make up WORDS, then stories are made of letters.

In this MENAGERIE we have stories, made of WORDS, MADE <u>FOR</u> all the LETTERS.

An Astronaut

A a

Edmund was an astronaut.

For ages he'd been training
to go on an adventure up into
space to meet some aliens.

Although there was a problem.

Space was about three hundred
and twenty-eight thousand,
four hundred and sixteen feet
above him...

...and Edmund had a fear of heights.

Anything over three feet in the air
was a bit much for him.

He had a long way to go.

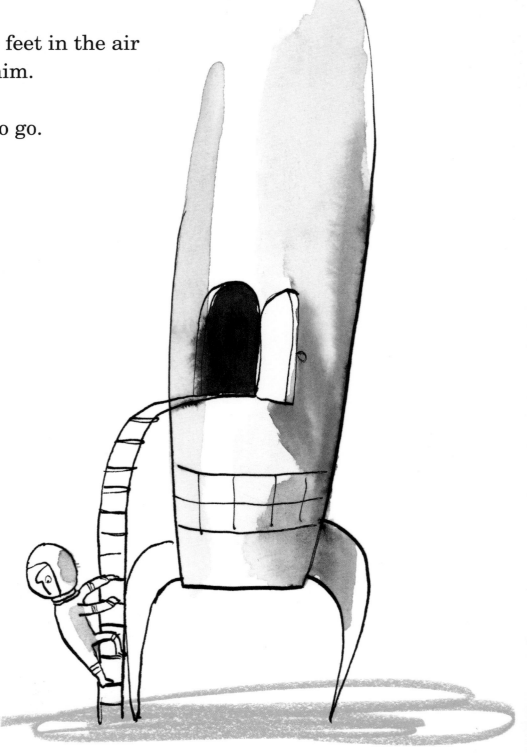

Another three hundred and twenty-eight
thousand, four hundred and thirteen feet
to be accurate.

BURNING A BRIDGE

B b

Bernard and Bob lived on either
side of a bridge and for years
had been battling each other for
reasons neither could remember.

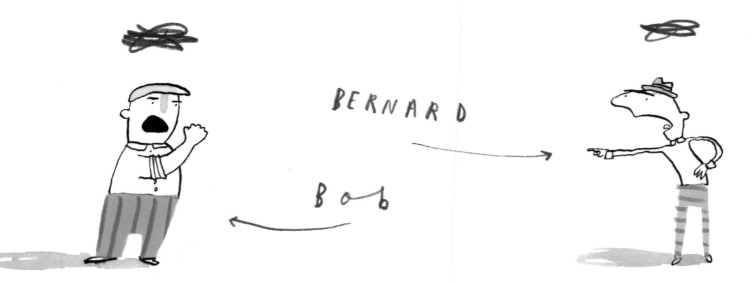

BERNARD

Bob

One day Bob decided to fix things
so Bernard couldn't bother him
anymore, by burning the bridge
between them.

But Bob learned an important lesson that day.

He needed the bridge to get back.

CUP in the
CUPBOARD

There's
TEA
in ME

Cup lived in the cupboard.
It was dark and cold in there
when the door was closed.

He dreamed of living over
by the window where he'd
have a clear view.

One afternoon, he decided
to go for it.

Unfortunately, he forgot that
the counter was a long way
down, and made of concrete.

Dd

Danger Delilah is a daredevil who laughs in the face of Death

and dances at the door of Disaster.

Nothing is too
dangerous and
she fears no one...

* DON'T TRY this at HOME

† GOOD LUCK TRYing this
if you can FIND a
DONKEY

...except her dad when she's late for dinner.

An
ENIGMA

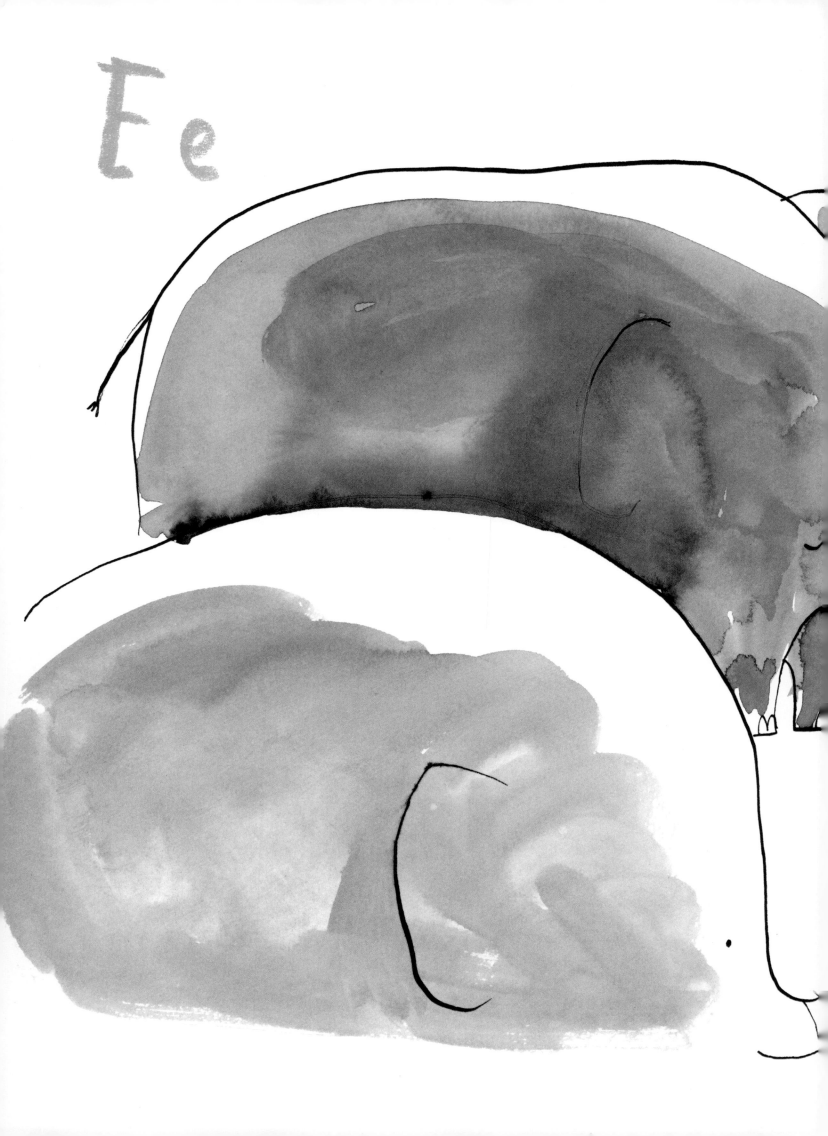

How many elephants can
you fit inside an envelope?

Turn to the letter N to find out...

Forever

F f

Ferdinand was out walking his
frog, when he came upon a hole.
A really big hole.

In fact it was the world's biggest
hole and it went on forever.

He dropped a penny in to see
how long it would take to hit
the bottom.

Would you believe me if
I told you it's still falling?

That's because
forever never ends...

Leopold Picard is a really great guard.

He'll guard anything he is given,
provided he is asked nicely enough.
(Good manners are very
important you know.)

GLACIER
this way →

NONE
SHALL
PASS
(without
asking
nicely)

His current assignment is a bit
boring. But he doesn't mind.

It's much better than his last one.

Half a
HOUSE

Helen lived in half a house.
The other half had fallen into
the sea during a hurricane
a year and a half ago.

Being lazy, and not owning
a hammer, she hadn't quite
got around to fixing it yet.
Which was fine…

...until the horrible day she
rolled out the wrong side of bed.

The
INVENTOR

I i

There once lived an ingenious inventor who invented many ingenious things.

His latest invention allowed him to observe iguanas in their natural habitat...

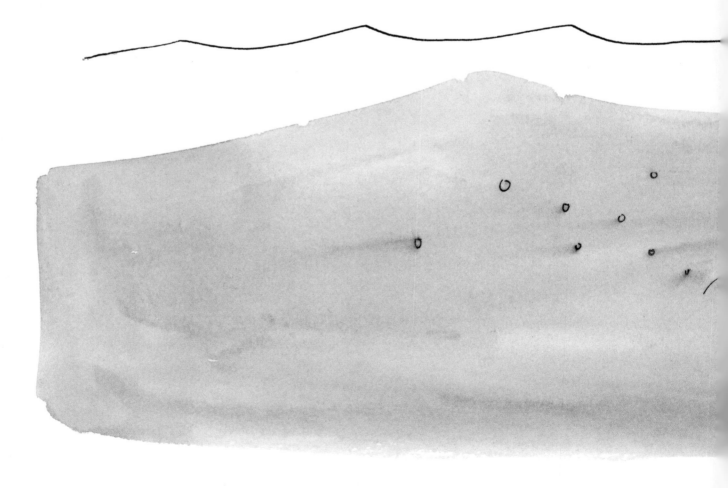

...incognito.

J

JELly

DOOR

J j

You can do all sorts
of things with jelly.

You can eat it.

You can throw it.

You can make stuff out of it.

That's what Jemima did.
She made her front door
out of jelly. That way, if she
ever left home without her
keys, she could just reach
in and grab them.

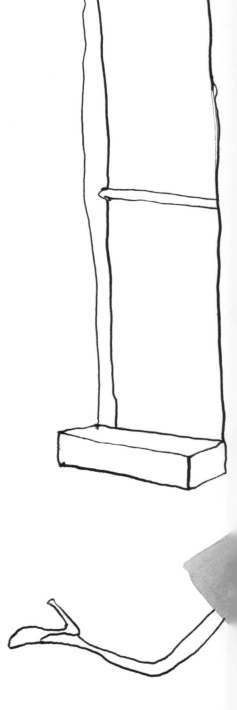

Of course, so could anyone else.

Because of that, the jelly door
never did catch on.

But, sure, who would be so
foolish as to forget their keys
in the first place?

The
KING

K k

The King of France
Went out for a dance
And forgot to bring along keys.

He got locked out
And sat about
All night with no sleep
And no cheese.

The
LUMBERJACK'S

Light

Jack Stack the Lumberjack has been struck by lightning one hundred and eleven times in his life so far. What lousy luck, you might think.

Well, the first few times were annoying, but he is actually beginning to like it now.

For one thing, he is so live with electricity...

...that he no longer needs
a plug for his light at night.

MADE of MATTER

Mm

Mary is made of matter.
So is her mother.
And her mother's moose.

In fact, matter makes up everything
from magnets and maps to
mountains and mattresses.

Mary discovered all of this the
marvellous day she got sucked
through a microscope and
became the size of a molecule. *

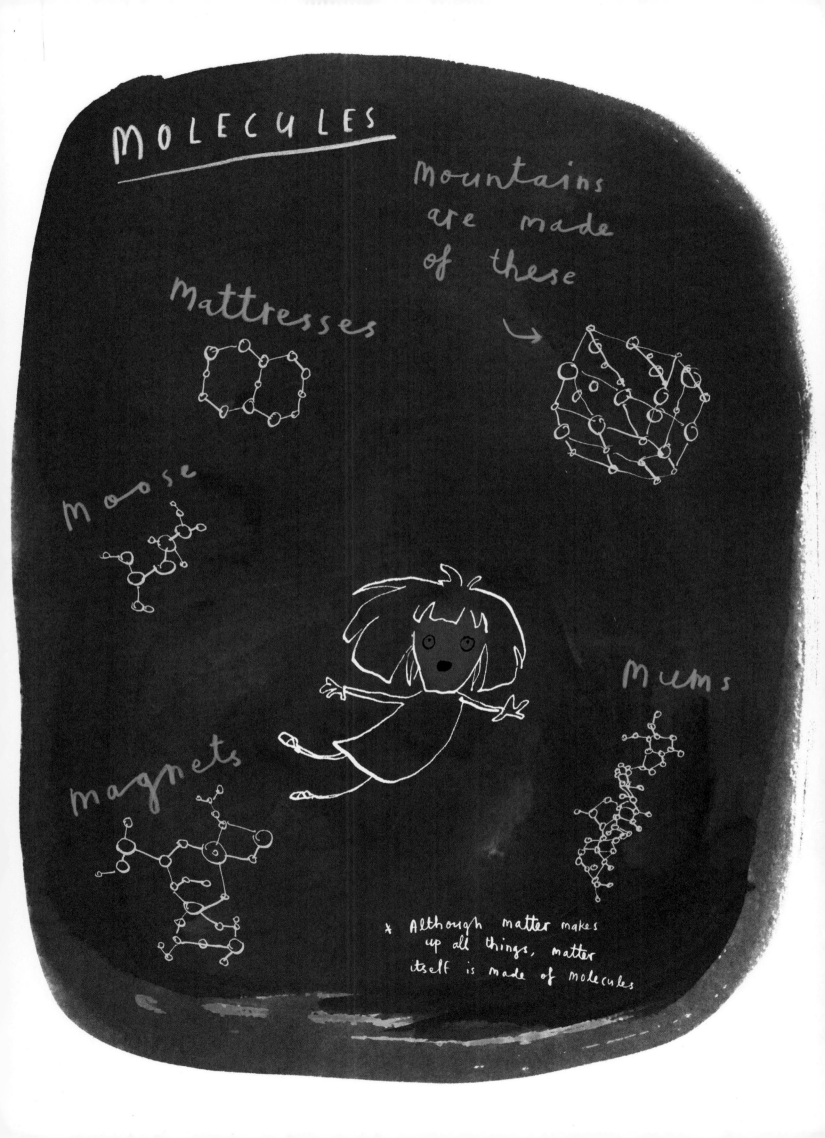

It's a minor miracle that they all made it back out of the microscope at their normal size again.

N

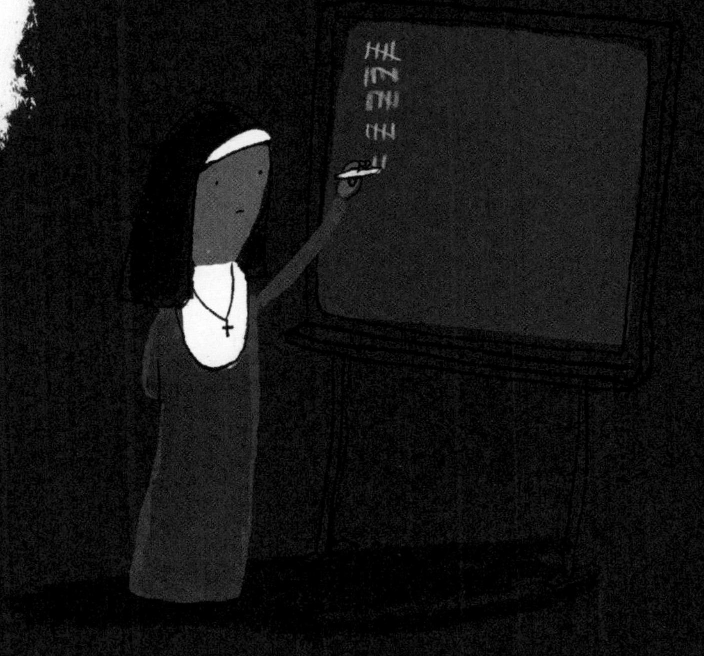

Nearly
NINE
Thousand

The answer to the enigma* is:
nearly nine thousand.

Sort of.

You could never actually fit
an elephant inside an envelope.

But you could fit nearly nine
thousand envelopes inside
an elephant.

*See the letter E

Then again, it depends on the size
of the envelope, so never say never.

ONWARD

Out on the ocean there
is an owl who rides on
the back of an octopus.

They search for problems.

They solve them.

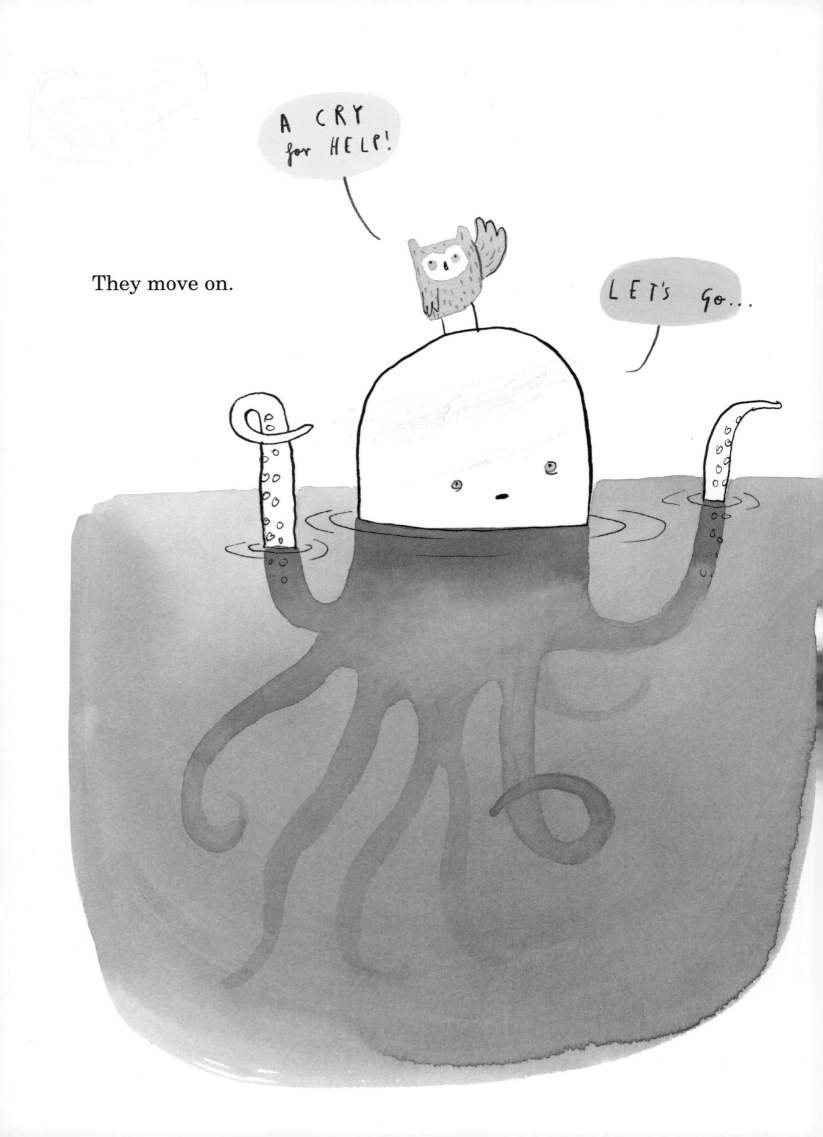

They move on.

A Puzzled
PARSNIP

Parsnips aren't known for
their intelligence, but this
one was particularly daft.

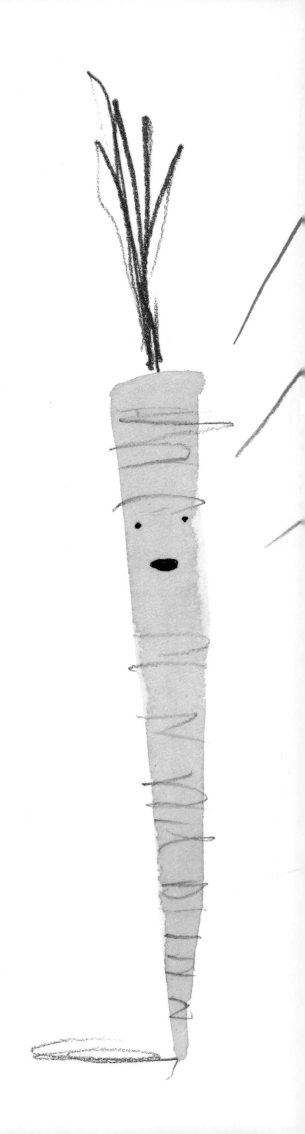

Point proven.

Q

The missing
Question

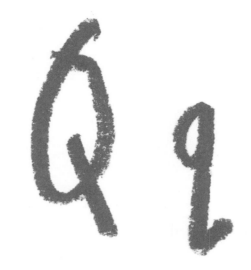

This story is supposed
to be about a question.

But I can't find it anywhere.

Do you know where it is?

ROBOTS

DON'T

LIKE

RAINclouds

Robots don't like rain clouds
So they steal them from the sky.

From everywhere and anywhere
That's why it's been so dry.

I'm sure you have been wondering,
What's with all this dust?

Well, robots don't like getting wet.
They don't do well with rust.

Sink
or
Swim

S s

This is the story of a regular
cucumber, who watched a
programme about sea cucumbers
and thought it might be a better
life for him.

That very evening, the regular
cucumber went to the shore
and, taking a last look around,
plunged into the sea.

However, never having tried
before, he hadn't realised he
couldn't swim, and sank straight
to the bottom.

He hasn't been heard from since.

But don't worry...

...the owl and the
octopus are on their way!

The TERRIBLE
TYPEWRITER

Tt

Not so long ago, and in a room
not so far away, sat a typewriter
and a terrified typist.

You see, whatever was written
on this particular typewriter,
however strange, had a terrible
habit of coming true.

It was only a few moments
before this typist's story...

...came to a tragic end.

UNDER GROUND

Unfortunately, Nigel wasn't very good at climbing.

The other monkeys laughed at him because he needed a ladder to get up the tree.

This upset Nigel,
so he used his ladder
to move underground.

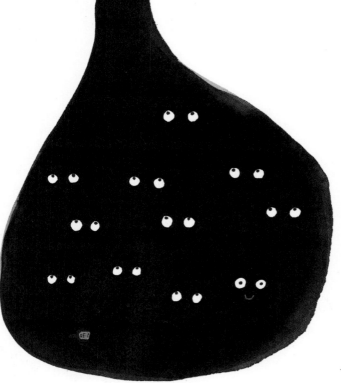

Turns out being underground
isn't so bad sometimes.

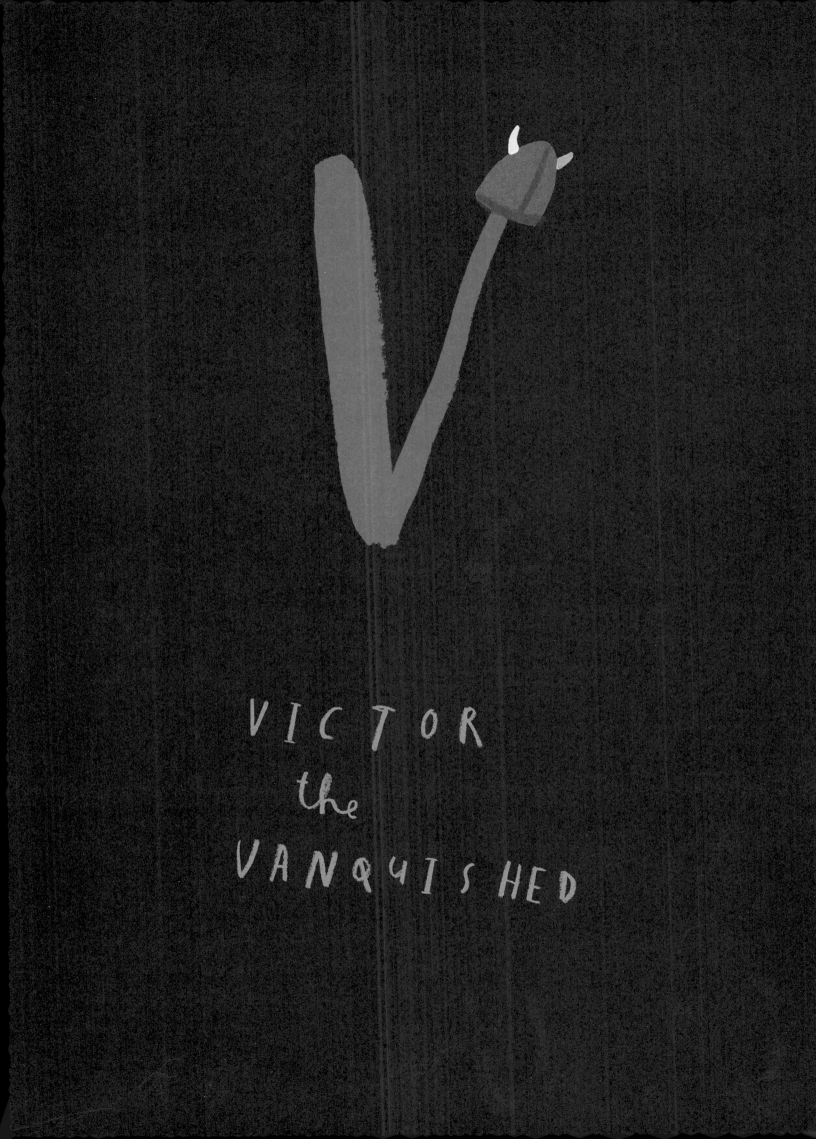

VICTOR
the
VANQUISHED

V v

Victor was used to being victorious.

But recently he was defeated
and retreated into hiding under
the stairs, where he now sits,
plotting his vengeance.

One day they'll all be very sorry.

The

WHIRAFFE

W w

The ingenious inventor had
a favourite invention of all –
the Whiraffe.

It had the head of a whisk
and the body of a giraffe.

They became great friends over
the years and enjoyed strawberries
and whipped cream.

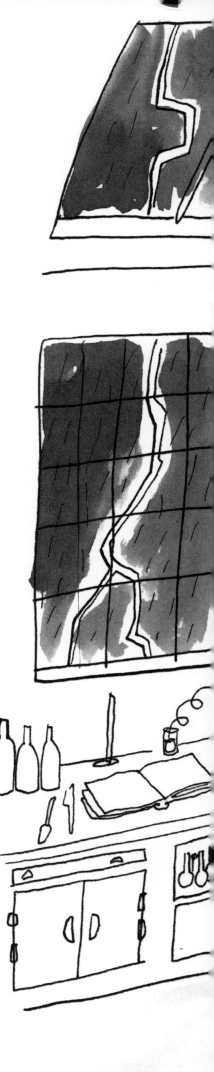

The Whiraffe, of course,
whipped the cream.

The CASE of the
MISSing X-RAY
SPECTACles

One terrible morning,
Xavier woke to discover that
his excellent pair of x-ray
spectacles had been stolen.

He knew exactly who to call…

What the owl and the octopus
knew, that the burglar did not,
was that an extra pair existed.

Y

A YETI, a YAK
and a YO-YO

A yeti up north
Bought a yo-yo of sorts
From a yak only yesterday.

But, here's the thing,

It didn't have string,

So this morning
He threw it away.

ZEPPELin

Edmund the astronaut
has made some progress.

He purchased a Zeppelin
and now drives a steady
four feet from the ground.

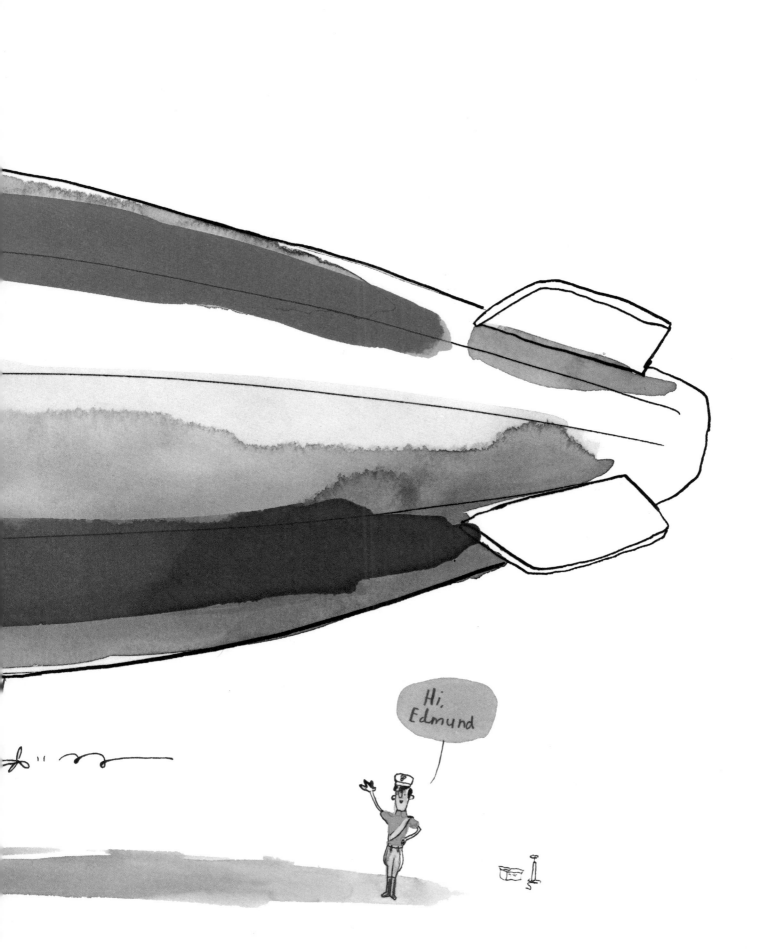

Only three hundred and twenty-eight thousand, four hundred and twelve to go.